Tips for Reading Together

Children learn best when reading is fun.

- Talk about the title and the pictures on the cover.
- Discuss what you think the story might be about.
- Read the story together, inviting your child to read as much of it as they can.
- Give lots of praise as your child reads, and help them when necessary.
- Try different ways of helping if they get stuck on a word. For example, get them to say the first sound of the word, or break it into chunks, or read the whole sentence again, trying to guess the word. Focus on the meaning.
- Have fun finding the hidden mice.
- Re-read the story later, encouraging your child to read as much of it as they can.

Children enjoy re-reading stories and this helps to build their confidence.

Have fun!

Find the 10 mice hidden in the pictures.

The Palace Statues

Written by Cynthia Rider

Illustrated by Alex Brychta

OXFORD
UNIVERSITY PRESS

The children put on a play called
The Golden Statue. Chip was the statue.
He had on a golden cloak and gold
face paint.

"I like this gold face paint," said
Anneena.

The magic key began to glow.

The magic took the children to a
palace. They saw a man talking to
a girl.

"Don't cry, Eva," he said.

"What's the matter?" asked Biff.

"This is my brother, Aran," said Eva. "He guards the golden statues in the palace."

"The statues all have jewels," said
Aran. "But someone is stealing the
jewels, and I *must* catch the robber."

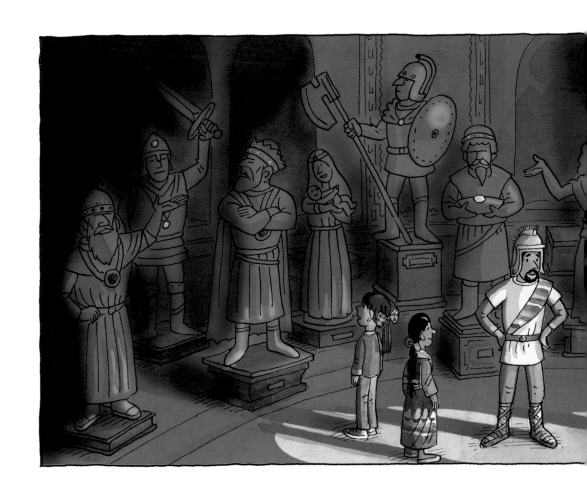

Aran showed the children the golden statues. "The robber might steal more jewels tonight," he said. "What can I do?"

Chip had an idea. "You can
dress up as a golden statue," he said.
"Then you can keep watch."

That night, Aran dressed up as a
golden statue.

"I'm glad we've got this gold face
paint," said Anneena.

Aran went into the statue room.
He stood in the deepest shadows.

"You need a jewel," said Eva. She
gave him her necklace, and went out.

Suddenly, a secret door slid open.
Two men crept into the room. They
took the rest of the jewels.

One of the men spotted Aran.
"I didn't see that statue last night,"
he said. "Let's get that necklace."

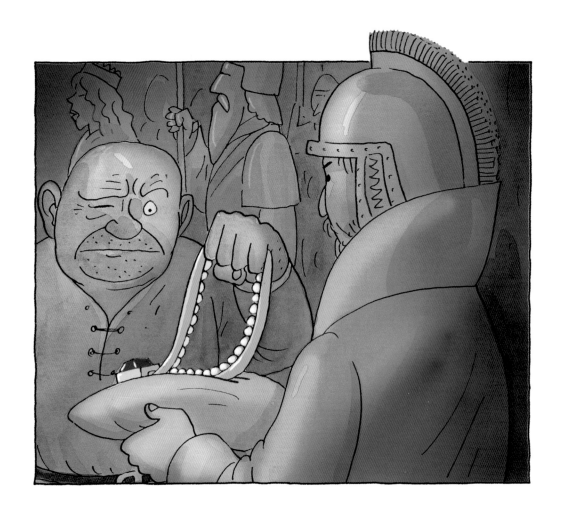

Aran held his breath as the man
grabbed the necklace.

At last, he heard a soft thud as the
secret door slid shut.

Aran called
the children. He
showed them the secret
door. They all crept down
some steps and along a shadowy
tunnel.

Suddenly, Biff tripped and fell.

"Who's there?" shouted the men.

"Run!" whispered Nadim. "Hide under the steps."

A robber came up to the steps.
He held up his lamp but the
children were as still as statues.

"There's nobody here," he said.

The men went into a dusty room.
The children followed them and
peeped round the door.

"There's another door!" said Aran.
"It must lead into the palace garden.
They might escape through that."

"I know what we can do," said Nadim, and he told the others his plan.

"That's a good idea," said Eva.

Eva raced back up the steps. She
told the guards to go to the garden
door. Then she ran back to the
others.

Aran marched stiffly into the
dusty room.

"Give me back my necklace!" he
roared, in a voice like thunder.

The robbers jumped up.

"Help! The statue is alive!" they screamed. They raced out of the garden door . . .

. . . and ran right into the guards!

The next day, Aran and Eva gave
the children a golden statue.

"Thank you for helping us," they
said. The magic key began to glow.

The magic took the children home.

"The statue looks just like Eva," said Nadim.

"Yes," said Chip. "And Anneena looks just like the statue!"

Think about the story

Why was Eva crying?

What was Nadim's plan?

How do you think the children felt when they were hiding?

How would you help someone who was crying?

Helping Aran

Help Aran to match the jewels to the statues.

Useful common words repeated in this story and other
books in the series.
began called children door face garden gave
idea might others room suddenly
Names in this story: Anneena Aran Biff Chip
Eva Nadim

More books for you to enjoy

Level 1: Getting Ready

Level 2: Starting to Read

Level 3: Becoming a Reader

Level 4: Building Confidence

Level 5: Reading with Confidence

OXFORD
UNIVERSITY PRESS

Great Clarendon Street,
Oxford OX2 6DP

Written by Cynthia Rider based
on original characters created by
Roderick Hunt and Alex Brychta
Text © Cynthia Rider 2008
Illustrations © Alex Brychta 2008
This edition published 2010

First published 2008

Read at Home Series Editors:
Kate Ruttle, Annemarie Young

British Library Cataloguing
in Publication Data available

ISBN: 9780198387718

10 9 8 7 6 5 4 3 2 1

Printed in China by Imago

Have more fun with Read at Home

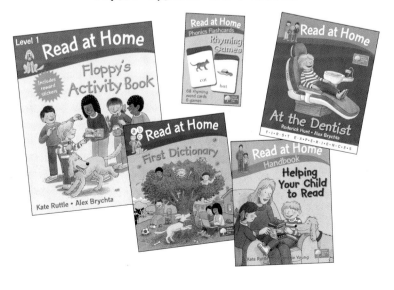

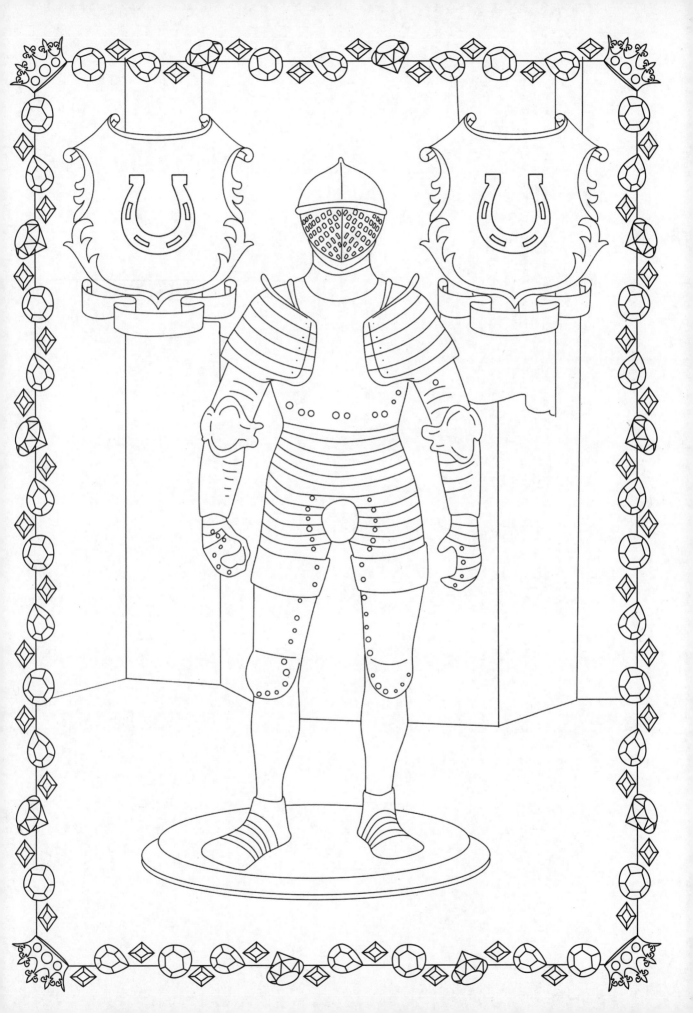